MY VAMPIRE HANDBOOK

A Parachute Press Book

PUBLISHED BY POCKET BOOKS

New York   London   Toronto   Sydney   Tokyo   Singapore

A MINSTREL PAPERBACK *Original*

 A Minstrel Paperback published by
POCKET BOOKS, a division of Simon & Schuster Inc.
1230 Avenue of the Americas, New York, New York 10020

Copyright © 1996 by Parachute Press, Inc.

MY VAMPIRE HANDBOOK WRITTEN BY NANCY E. KRULIK

All rights reserved, including the right to reproduce
this book or portions thereof in any form whatsoever.
For information address Pocket Books, 1230 Avenue
of the Americas, New York, NY 10020

ISBN: 0-671-00345-3

First Minstrel Books printing October 1996

10 9 8 7 6 5 4 3 2 1

FEAR STREET is a registered trademark of
Parachute Press, Inc.

A MINSTREL BOOK and colophon are registered trademarks of
Simon & Schuster Inc.

Cover art by John Youssi

Printed in the U.S.A.

TERRIFYING TABLE OF CONTENTS

You Have Been Chosen....

Good eee-vening!

I am Count Humphrey Ved. I hang out with all the ghosts and ghouls on Fear Street. And now you will too—because I have chosen *you* to become a vampire!

Whoa! Hold it, kid! Don't run away screaming just yet! Think of all the *fang*-tastic things vampires get to do!

Vampires can sleep all day and stay up all night long! Vampires never go to school or do homework. (When would you ever get away with that as a *human* kid?) Plus, if they want to go somewhere, *poof!* Vampires can simply turn into a bat and fly off. And you know vampires have the best clothes. Wearing all black is so cool!

What? You're still not sure you want to be a vampire? I'm sure you've got it in you. I choose my victims—uh, *friends*—carefully. Haven't made a bad choice in six hundred years! (Of course, you *are* a little puny. From the looks of you, you could be my first big mistake.)

Come with me and I'll show you how *you* can look, think, talk, and party like a vampire! You're going to *love* it!

Read on to let the scary stuff begin!

Chapter One

FRIGHTENING VAMPIRE FACTS!

So, kid, have you ever seen a vampire?

Actually, you probably wouldn't know if you had. We vampires are hard to pick out in a crowd. That's because we look just like humans.

But if you look closely, you'll be able to separate the living from the *undead*.

HOW TO SPOT A VAMPIRE

1. Vampires won't go anywhere near garlic.
2. Vampires can often take away a person's voice, strength, and beauty.
3. Vampires come out only after dark.
4. Some vampires are born, not made. The seventh son of the seventh son in a family can be a vampire—without ever being bitten.
5. Vampires can't see their reflections in a mirror.
6. Vampires can't cross running water.
7. Vampires can't stand to hear bells ringing.
8. Vampires can't eat or drink anything but the blood of the living.
9. Vampires are notorious liars. In fact, they rarely tell the truth.
10. Vampires can't enter any place they have not been invited into.

Being a vampire is great—but it does have a few drawbacks.

Someone could get the big idea that they want to get rid of you. And there are a few ways that they can! But your immortality is safe with me, kid. Just look at this list of things to beware of, and you can stop the humans from taking a bite out of *you!*

VAMPIRES BEWARE!

1. Garlic is bad. Really bad. Some humans rub garlic on their doors, windows, chimneys, and keyholes to keep vampires away. But then, *anyone* would stay away from a house like that! P.U.!

2. Any exposure to sunlight will turn a vampire into dust immediately. Talk about your sunburn! Always be sure to wear your shades—and some heavy-duty sun block—whenever you venture out of your coffin!

3. Humans have been known to spread poppy seeds on a path leading from a vampire's coffin into town. We vampires can't resist counting little things. (Maybe that's why they call us Counts!) We're drawn to count the seeds. It takes so long that the sun comes up without our realizing it. And you know what that means—vampire toast!

4. Most humans know the only sure way to kill a vampire is to drive a wooden stake through his heart. (Oooh! Just the word *stake* sends shivers through my fangs!) But fear not. Most humans don't know that they can't use *any* stake. It must be made from the wood of a wild rosebush or an ash tree.

A Little Vampire History

When you think of vampires, who's the first guy
that comes to your mind? That's right—the one and
only Count Dracula! He's the biggest, baddest blood-
sucker around. (And he's every vampire's hero!)
Some people don't believe there ever was a
Dracula, but actually—

Dracula Lived!

That's right. There really was a Count Dracula!
Historians say the real-life Dracula was a cruel
and frightening count who lived in *Rumania* during
the mid-1400s. The Count's full name was Vlad
Dracula. "Dracul" means "devil" or "dragon" in
Rumanian. So Dracula was a fitting name for such
a stupendously scary guy!

Vlad Dracula was considered the most *blood-
thirsty* guy around. That's because he killed most
of his enemies in a terrifically terrible way—by
cutting off their heads. Then he left the heads outside
on stakes—as food for birds!

But poor Count Dracula's story has a sad end.
When he was 45 years old, Vlad Dracula's enemies

cut off *his* head. (Oh, the poor guy. I'm getting all choked up. Hey, kid, got any tissues?) Dracula's headless body was buried in an unmarked grave off the coast of Rumania.

Did Dracula rise from the grave to become one of the most terrifying vampires ever? No one is really sure. That's because to this day, no one can find his body! We do know that some Rumanians still fear him. Rumanian grown-ups tell kids who misbehave, "Behave, or Dracula will get you!" Also, many people claim to have spotted the fantastic, fearsome Count.

One place Dracula has been spotted is in books. Bram Stoker wrote his book, *Dracula,* in 1897. People still read the book today. (That's because the Count is so scary, he leaves people *screaming* for more!)

Bram Stoker's Dracula was tall and thin. He wore plenty of black, and was usually seen in a long cape. (Terrifying *and* fashionable! What a guy!)

According to Bram Stoker, Dracula had flaring nostrils and long, sharp teeth. Plus, this vampire could perform some really neat tricks—like changing himself into a bat, a wolf, or a misty fog.

Legend has it that Bram Stoker saw Dracula in a dream. (I bet it was more like a nightmare!) That dream inspired Stoker to write one of the scariest stories ever told—and make vampires the subject of people's nightmares all over the world!

Lights! Camera! Fangs!

It's no wonder Dracula is every vampire's hero. Not only is he the main character in one of the scariest books ever written—he's also been in the movies!

The first movie about him was made in Germany. It was a silent film called *Nosferatu.*

Americans got into the vampire act a few years later with a silent film called *London After Midnight.* It starred a famous actor named Lon Chaney.

But the person most famous for playing the cruel Count was a Hungarian actor named Bela Lugosi. Lugosi was born near Transylvania (where Bram Stoker's Dracula made *his* horrific home), so Lugosi had the right accent. He even took to sleeping in a nice, comfy coffin—although he claimed it was because the hard surface helped ease his back pain. (But make no mistake. Lugosi didn't have the privilege of being a real vampire—like us!)

Vampires Are Everywhere!

Dracula wasn't the only person famous for being a vampire. How about this cruel Countess?

Countess Elizabeth Bathory lived in Hungary about 100 years after Dracula's death. The Countess and Dracula had a lot in common. For instance, they were both notoriously nasty. And they both had many enemies.

The Countess took great pride in her looks, but as she grew older, she was afraid her beauty was fading. This made her even more mean than she already was.

One day she hit one of her maids. The Countess hit the maid so hard that she cut the maid's cheek. Blood from the cut dripped onto Countess Bathory's hand. Soon, the vain Countess was convinced that the spot where the blood had been on her hand looked firmer and younger than the rest of her skin.

From that moment on, the Countess believed the blood of young women would bring back her beauty. Over the next 10 years, she killed many young women to fill up her blood bank.

Vampires Around the World!

Not many people know that there are different *types* of vampires. Over the centuries, people from many different countries have agreed that vampires exist. But they have *disagreed* on what shape and size vampires are.

Want to meet some of these creepy creatures? Come along . . . if you dare!

EUROPE

Some Rumanian people once believed in a vampire known as Varcolac. Varcolac was so large, he could eat the sun and the moon!

When an eclipse made the sun or the moon disappear in the sky, people thought Varcolac had eaten it! (Talk about a vampire with a big appetite!)

Not everyone thinks that vampires are frightening. Many people in Central Europe believed that, after a man died, he would return to his family as a sort of "good vampire." He would spend his nights helping with the housework and chatting with his wife.

CHINA

It would be a lot easier to spot a vampire in China than in Europe. While the Europeans believed that vampires looked pretty much like humans (but much cooler, of course), the Chinese believed that vampires were covered with white hair, and had long claws. Boy, *those* vampires sure stood out in a crowd.

MALAYSIA

Some Malaysians tell stories of a female vampire called Polong. Polong was even harder to spot than Count Dracula. That's because she took the form of a tiny girl about the size of your pinky!

Other Malaysians believed in a type of vampire *pet*. They called the vampire "bajang." Bajang looked very much like a cat. If this vampire wanted to go into a house, it would sit outside the door and start to meow. If the people inside the house wanted some vampire company, all they had to do was open the door and let the cat in.

Why would these silly humans *want* a vampire in their house? (Good question, kid. You're beginning to show some promise!) They wanted the bajang because having one gave the family a lot of power. If they chose to, they could tell the bajang to do mean things to people they didn't like.

SOUTH AMERICA

Today, most people don't really believe in vampires. (Boy, are they in for a surprise when they meet me!) But in a few far-off places, belief still lingers. As recently as the 1960s, a man in Argentina was punished for biting the necks of 15 people. Although he said he didn't know what made him do it, many of the townsfolk did. They were sure he was a vampire!

Fill in the Fright!

Those vampire stories were totally terrific, weren't they? Well, since you're about to become a vampire yourself, it's time to write a scary story about *you*!

Hey, what's the matter, kid? Suddenly you don't look so good. Oh! I get it. You're not a great writer. Well, don't worry. Just get some of your friends to help you.

Directions: Gather some of your friends together. Have someone other than yourself hold this book—so that no one (including you) can see what the story is about. No peeking!

Have the friend who's holding the book read the description beneath each blank. (The descriptions are the words in tiny letters.) Then it's up to you and your friends to call out suggestions for filling in that blank. Decide on one of the suggestions and have the person holding the book write it in. Do the same for every blank.

Once all of the blanks are filled in, go back and read the entire story out loud.

It was a cold and _____

any adjective

night. In the distance, I could hear the flapping of

bat's _____ as they flew

an animal body part

through the trees. The sound was oddly soothing,

like the music of beating _____.

musical instruments

I poured myself a glass of _____

liquid

and took a small sip. I looked up in the sky and saw

the _____. It was almost

a noun

full, and looked lovely reflected in the shallow

_____. But alas, the calmness

another liquid

was soon to _____.

a verb

I was jolted into reality by the sound of a

woman's shrill _____. It sounded as

a noise

though she were in real _____.

another noun

I _____ in the

a verb

10

direction of the noise. I found the woman lying

facedown in the _____.

I turned her over and discovered _____

holes in her _____.

 I was shocked! I had, of course, heard stories

about Count _____

being a vampire. But I thought it was just the

ranting of crazy _____.

Now I knew it was true. When the

_____ went down and the

_____ could be seen in the

sky, the Count went out _____

for human _____.

 I had to protect myself. I knew there was

only one thing that could ward the count off. And

that was smelly, stinky, _____

_____. Vampires can't stand the stuff.
_{a spice}

So, I hopped in my _____,
_{a method of transportation}

ran off to the nearest _____,
_{a fast-food restaurant}

and ordered a pizza with extra _____.
_{same spice as above}

I sank my teeth into a slice. By the time I

finished, I knew my breath must smell really

_____.
_{an adjective}

My plan worked perfectly! Count

_____ never bothered with
_{same name as in title}

me.

Unfortunately, neither did anyone else!

THE END

Bat Facts!

Once you're a vampire, you'll be able to turn into a bat and fly! So you'll need some important bat facts.

Did you know? . . .

Humans are in the same family as bats. And not just *undead* humans like us vampires. Live ones too! Both bats and people are mammals. That means they both feed their babies milk that is made in the body of the mother.

Vampire bats really exist! While a few vampire bats have taken a nip from a human now and again, for the most part, these small, reddish-brown animals sink their razor-sharp teeth into cows and other livestock. The bite itself is harmless and heals quickly. But many vampire bats carry a dangerous disease called rabies. So there's still a very good reason for humans to stay away from vampire bats.

Most bats are useful to humans. They eat lots of annoying, harmful insects.

Most bats are not blind. Bats can see, though sight is not their strongest sense. Bats get around using their sense of hearing. They make a high-pitched noise, which humans cannot hear. The sound waves from that noise bounce off objects that are in the bat's flight path. The echoing sound comes back to the bat and warns it that something is in its way.

Bats sleep upside down. When daylight comes, they hang from the ceilings of their homes by their feet and wrap their wings around their bodies.

Chapter Two

VAMPIRE TRICKS TO DRIVE YOUR FRIENDS BATTY!

Now that you know your vampire facts, the second vampire lesson you'll need to learn is how to be sneaky. After all, humans are not *completely* stupid. They don't just walk right up to a vampire and offer their necks. Every good vampire has a few tricks up his or her sleeves for fooling humans.

Here are a few for you to try.

Spooky Supernatural Strength!

Vampires are the strongest beings alive. Now you can fool your friends into thinking you have bulging vampire biceps! Here's how.

To do this trick, you will need:
• a paper towel   • some water

Here's the setup:
1. Hold two opposite corners of the paper towel.

Twist the paper towel from the corners until it's rolled up nice and tight and looks like a rope.
2. Ask your friend to hold the paper towel by the two ends and try to rip it by pulling the ends outward.
3. After your friend has tried (and failed) to pull the paper towel apart, take the towel from him/her. Tell your friend that only a vampire is strong enough to perform such an incredible feat.
4. Hold the paper towel at either end and pull. For you, the towel will break easily!

Here's the vampire secret:
1. While your friend is huffing and puffing, trying to get the paper towel to rip, you excuse yourself and slip away.
2. Wet your fingertips with water.
3. When you return to take the paper towel, hold it in the middle with your wet fingertips. The paper towel will absorb the water, and become soft in the middle.
4. Then hold the paper towel at either end and pull. It will now rip easily!

Dracula's Finger Has Been Found

While it's true that no one can find Dracula's body, someone *has* found one of his fingers. At least it appears that someone has. And that sneaky someone is *you!*

To do this trick you will need:
• a small box with a lid (about the size of a
  cardboard jewelry box)
• scissors
• five cotton balls

Here's the setup:
1. Cut a small hole in the bottom of the box, close
to one of the sides. Make sure the hole is big
enough for your pointer finger to fit through.
2. Put cotton around the hole inside the box.
3. Stick your finger through the hole and close the
lid on the box.

Here's the trick:
1. Gather a group of friends around. Tell them
you've stumbled on an amazing discovery—
Dracula's finger, which hasn't been seen since the
gloriously gruesome Count died in the 1400s. (If
anyone asks you where you found it, just say "I
can't quite put my finger on it!")
2. Let the box rest in your hand, but be slick about
it. Use your other hand to hold the part of the box
that faces your audience. This will hide the finger
that is sticking through the bottom of the box.
3. Now hold the box up. Use the finger in the box to
push the lid off. Do it slowly so it looks as though
the lid is rising by itself. Imagine your audience's
shock as they see Dracula's finger moving all by
itself!

The Vampire-Bat-in-the-Bag Trick

Convince your friends that you can trap a vampire. It's easy.

To do this trick you will need:
- a brown paper bag   • two of your fingers.

Here's the trick:
1. Gather some friends in your room. Let them hang out. . . for a while. Then, suddenly, stop dead (or is that *undead?*) in your tracks. Here's where your sneakiness comes in.
2. Tell your visitors that you think there's a vampire bat circling your room. Then tell them not to worry. After all, you are a well-known Vampire Bat Catcher!
3. Hold the bag open. As soon as you do, it will snap shut . . . with a loud bang. You've caught the bat. . . or so your friends will think.

Here's the vampire secret:
Hold the open edge of the bag between your thumb and middle fingers. Snap your fingers with the bag between them. The snap will sound extra loud when your thumb hits the paper. Then quickly close the bag as if you just sacked the bat.

What do you do if anyone wants to see the bat inside the bag? Tell them they must be nuts! After all, they don't want that bat to escape again, do they?

Vampire in Iron Chains

Do you have a friend who is really scared of the undead? Someone who truly believes in vampires? Well, find someone like that, and you've found the perfect *victim* for this joke. (It's a gag with real bite!)

Here's what you do:
1. Walk up to your victim. Then back away with fear in your eyes. Shout out, "Are you a vampire *in chains?"*
2. Your friend is certain to give you a real evil eye. Then he or she will probably say, "No. I'm *not* a vampire in chains."
3. That's your cue! Let out a bloodcurdling cry and announce to anyone nearby, "Not in chains? Help! There's a vampire *on the loose!"* Then run off as fast as you can, leaving your friend's blood boiling!

Fang-twisters!

You'll want to get used to having those sharp, pointy teeth—or you'll stab yourself in the tongue! (Ouch!) Try these tough tongue twisters. Say each one three times fast. Then try them on a favorite fiend . . . oops, friend!

Red blood, blue blood.

•

**Five fanged fellows
fought fearlessly.**

•

**The careless count
closed Cleo's coffin.**

•

**The vain vampire was
vulnerable to vipers.**

•

**Dracula's dreaded
drink drained Drake.**

Super Spooky Joke Stop!

Whew! I've already taught you so much about being a vampire. But there is still much to learn—like how to make vampire friends! The best way to start is by telling a few vampire jokes. I, Count Humphrey Ved, will share my favorite vampire jokes with you!

What is Count Dracula's favorite sport?
Skin diving!

What kind of coat does Count Dracula wear on a rainy day?
A wet one!

Why did the doctor tell the vampire to get plenty of rest?
He was dead on his feet!

What is a Vampire's favorite holiday?
Fangs-giving!

Vampire Preview!

You're not quite ready to be a vampire yet, but you can still see how you'll look in your new, immortal life! All you need is the special vampire makeup and fangs that come with this book. Remember to use only the makeup in this kit to create your new, super-scary self!

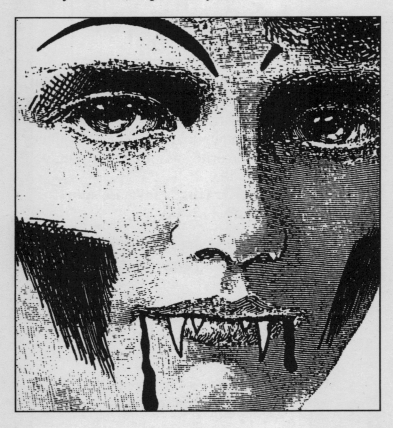

Here's how to transform your face:

1. Cover your whole face with the white makeup in this kit. (One of the coolest things about us vampires is our milky-white complexion. No suntan for us, thank you!)

2. Apply the red makeup in this kit to your lips to give them that attractive blood-red color.

3. Apply the black makeup from this kit to your cheekbones for that "just-rose-from-the-coffin" look.

4. Use more of the black makeup to draw in arching eyebrows *above* your own eyebrows. (For extra-scary eyes, have an adult help you put the black makeup on your eyelids too.)

5. A couple of drops of blood leaking from the corners of your mouth will polish off your fearsome face. Use the fake blood in this kit. (Real blood would simply be too messy right now!)

6. Once you have painted your face, it's time to take a bite out of life! Place the fangs over your real teeth.

Wow, kid! You look absolutely fang-tastic!

Chapter Three

AMAZING ACTIVITIES TO SINK YOUR FANGS INTO!

Are you bored? Looking for a few activities you can sink your fangs into? Well, you've come to the right place!

Blood Type Lingo!

Let's face it. A vampire is really just a count or countess with a big secret. A bloodcurdling secret, you might say.

Do you have a secret? Want to keep it that way? Then reveal your secret only to someone you trust. And do it in this blood-type language.   All you have to do is add the blood-type letters . . . a, b, and o!

Here's how you do it:

Choose a one syllable word. Drop the first consonant of the syllable. Say it. Then take the consonant that you dropped and add "abo" to it. The word "bat," for example, would become "at-babo."

If a word has two or more syllables, treat each syllable as a separate word. The word "vampire" would be "am-vabo ire-pabo."

If a word starts with a vowel and is only one syllable, just add abo to it. That means the word eat would be eat-abo.

If a word begins with a blend (two consonants working together to make one sound), treat the two letters as one. So, the name "Dracula" would become "ac-Drabo u-abo a-labo."

Can you figure out these abo sentences?

1. I-abo ant-wabo o-tabo ink-drabo our-yabo ood-blabo!
2. e-Thabo ount-cabo as-habo one-gabo at-babo y-tabo.
3. Ood-blabo is-abo icker-thabo an-thabo ater-wabo, and-abo as-tabo i-tabo er-abo, oo-tabo!
4. Ood-gabo ob-jabo, id-kabo! Ouabo-yabo acked-crabo e-thabo ode-cabo!

Freaky, Frightening Flicks!

Picture it. You've spent the whole night being a real pain in the neck. Now you're tucking yourself in for a long, comfortable day in the coffin. But you're not quite ready for sleep. No problem! We vampires have a few great movies we love to watch as we unwind from a long night's work. I hear that humans like these movies almost as much as vampires. And that humans usually get them at their local video store.

But humans your age should watch these frightening flicks with an adult. They can be *super* scary!

Dracula: There may be lots of videos with this name on the box. But be sure you rent the 1931 classic starring Bela Lugosi! As far as I, Count Humphrey Ved, am concerned, he's the only movie Count that counts! (Not rated.)

Son of Dracula: This film was made in 1943. Its story is not set in Transylvania like most Dracula movies. Instead it's set in the southern United States. An odd fellow named Alucard (spell it backwards and you'll get the joke) moves to a small town in the hopes of sampling some southern blood. (Not rated.)

Love at First Bite*:* Count Dracula, bored of Transylvania, comes to Manhattan to enjoy a bit of "night life." (1979, PG)

The Monster Squad: In this movie, made in 1987, Count Dracula searches for a magic amulet that will give him the ultimate power over good and evil. (Go Count!) To help him search for the amulet, he enlists the help of his buddies—the Mummy, Frankenstein, the Wolfman, and Gill-Man. The only thing standing between Drac and the amulet is the Monster Squad—a group of kids ready to battle whatever the Count throws their way! (PG-13.)

Abbott and Costello Meet Frankenstein: I know what you're thinking. What does Frankenstein have to do with teaching you to be a vampire—right kid? Well trust me, this very funny film, made in 1948, has more than its share of the Big D—that's right, Dracula. Plus it has a few *bonus* monsters—like the Wolfman. Yeah, this movie is a real howl! (Not rated.)

Dracula vs. Frankenstein: In this 1971 film, Dracula hates Dr. Frankenstein. He really, really hates him. So why has he been seen around town with him? Because the two have made a deal that will provide the count with a never-ending supply of blood. Sounds like a good deal to me! Yum, yum! (PG)

My Best Friend Is a Vampire: In 1988, a high school kid finds that turning into a vampire can take a real bite out of your grades. (PG)

Super Spooky
Joke Stop #2!

More frightfully funny jokes!

**What do you get when you cross
Count Dracula with a scarf?**
A real pain in the neck!

**Why did the vampire
cross the road?**
To bite someone on the other side.

**What is a vampire's
favorite candy?**
An all-day sucker!

**Where do vampires
go swimming?**
In the Dead Sea!

Chapter Four

THROW A FANG-TASTIC FIESTA!

The moon is out. The sky is cloudy. Dead leaves skitter across the sidewalk in the cool October air. It's the perfect night for a vampire to party! What's that? You say you're not quite sure how to throw a really frightening festival for the undead? Well, never fear! You'll get all the information here!

You're Invited!

The key to any good party is to set the tone, even before your guests arrive! In this case, it means sending scary invitations. Your vampire buddies will just eat them up! And these batty invitations are in exactly the right *vein!*

You will need:
- scissors
- glue
- black construction paper
- plain white paper

Here's what you do:
1. Copy the shape you see on the next page onto

black construction paper. (You might want to make yours a little bigger than this one.)

2. Draw a bat on the invitation. You can copy this one or make your own, but be sure the bat's head and wings are in the same place as this bat's.

3. Cut a 1- by 2-inch square of the plain white paper. Glue the paper between the bat wings as shown in the picture.

4. Write the following on the white paper:

> *You are invited to a Fang-Tastic Vampire*
> *Bash at _____'s house.*
> *Date: _____ Time: _____*

5. Carefully fold the bat's head down toward the white paper as shown.

6. Then fold the invitation in half.

When your friends open the card, the bat's head will pop out for a good scare!

Enter at Your Own Risk!

The *only* place for a vampire to party is in a haunted castle. What's that, kid? You say you don't live in a haunted castle?

Wanna bet? Just follow my instructions and you'll have the creepiest castle this side of Transylvania.

You will need:
- sheets
- scissors
- black construction paper
- a roll of clear tape
- cotton balls
- a tape recorder

Here's what you do:
1. Remember, you're not a vampire yet. So first, ask your parents' permission to turn your room into a haunted castle. (Some grown-ups just don't like having ghosts, spiders, and bats all over their house. Don't ask me why.) Once you have permission, you can get started.
2. Before your guests arrive, cover all the furniture in your party room with sheets.
3. Cut out bats from the black paper. Follow the picture on the next page or create some bats of your own. Tape the bats to the windows, doors, and walls.

4. Hang up lots of spider webs. You can make webs by stretching out balls of cotton until they are stringy. Tape the webs all over the room.

5. Use your tape recorder to record all kinds of creepy sounds. You can scream, squeak, or even say vampire-y things such as "Good Eee-evening," or "I vant to suck your blood."

6. Turn out the lights and wait for your guests to arrive. When the doorbell rings, turn on your spooky tape. Let the horrors begin!

It's scary! It's petrifying! It's absolutely perfect!

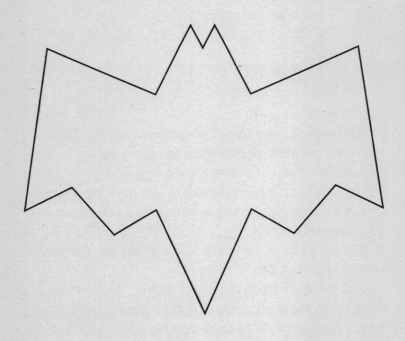

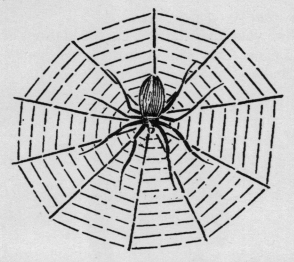

Now that all your ghoulish friends have arrived at your haunted castle, you need to have some really great games to keep the party *alive*. Try these to please your vampire guests.

Transfusion Confusion!
The bloodcurdling ice-breaker game!

Sometimes, even vampires need a little help getting to know one another. Here's an easy way to help the undead get to know one another.

You will need:
• red construction paper
• scissors
• black markers

Here's what you do:

1. Before your guests arrive, cut blood drops out of the red paper. They should be the same shape as the figure below—but much bigger.

2. Using the black marker, write blood types on the drops. The blood types are A+, B+, AB+, O+, A-, B-, AB-, and O-. You don't have to use all the blood types if you don't have enough guests. Just be sure you make two blood drops for every blood type you've used.

3. As your guests arrive, hand them a blood drop. When everyone has arrived (and gone through your haunted castle) it's time to play the game.

4. Tell your friends to wander around the room, looking for the vampire that shares his or her blood type.

The matching blood-type vampires must stick together to play the game on the next page.

The Great Bat Wing Relay Race

Here's what you do:

1. Have your guests line up at a starting line in groups of two.
2. Everybody must crouch down.
3. Teammates must link arms.
4. When you say "Go," the teammates must walk as fast as they can to the finish line. The trick is, everyone playing must walk in the crouched position— and they can't unlink their arms.
5. Any team that falls or lets go of one another's arms must go back to the starting line and begin again.

Watch everyone's silly walk as they race to the finish line! It's a real *scream!*

What's in the Coffin?

A memory game.

• • •

Here's what you do:

1. Before the party, fill a shoe box with at least ten different items. The items can be anything you want: pencils, crayons, pretzels, shoelaces, etc. Or you can use creepy things such as plastic spiders and your vampire fangs from this kit. (Just no garlic, please!)

2. During the party, give each of your guests the chance to look at the items in the box. Once everyone has studied the box, cover it up and hand out paper and pencils.

3. Ask your guests to write down every item in the box that they can remember.

• • •

The guest who correctly remembers the most items, wins.

The Scary Story Circle

With this game, the frights go on and on.

You will need:
• a flashlight

Here's what you do:

1. Ask your friends to sit in a circle. Turn out the lights.

2. Decide who will go first. Hand that guest the flashlight. The first player shines the flashlight under his or her chin and begins to make up a scary story. He/she can tell as much or as little of the story as he/she chooses. When he/she has told a bit of the story, he/she passes the flashlight to the next player.

3. The next player picks up the story where the first player left off. Keep going around and around, making sure everyone has had at least one chance to add something to the terrifying tale.

37

FANG-TASTIC FOODS!

Since you're not a vampire yet, you can't drink blood. But until then, there are some special treats you can serve at your party. These are recipes that have a true Transylvanian flavor!

A Blood-Red Sipper!

This scrumptious sipper is not a pain in the neck to make!

You will need:
- 3 cups milk
- 1 cup cranberry juice
- a blender (If you've never used one, ask an adult to help you.)
- 3 scoops vanilla ice cream

Here's what you do:
1. Pour the milk and the juice into the blender. Put the lid tightly on the blender and blend until well-mixed.
2. Add ice cream. Place the lid on tightly and blend again until the mixture is creamy.
3. Pour the sippers into tall glasses. Ask your friends to join you in an *a-b*-solutely delicious blood-red refreshment!

Sink Your Fangs into This!

Here's a tasty treat that's food and a game—all in one! Plus, it will get your fangs in shape for your first vampire feeding!

You will need:
• one bowl for each of your guests
• an ice-cream scooper
• strawberry ice cream
• strawberry sauce

Here's what you do:
1. Give each guest a bowl containing one scoop of strawberry ice cream topped with the blood-red strawberry sauce.
2. Have your guests sit with their hands behind their backs.
3. When you say "Go," the players must eat the scoop of ice cream—without using any spoons or their hands. Only fangs are allowed.
4. The first one to finish the scoop wins!
(Just a tip, kid. Be sure to have lots of paper towels and napkins handy. No vampire would ever want to be seen with blood dripping from their fangs!)

A Silver Screen Vampire Skit

Now's your chance. You've come this far—it's time to show off how much you can act like a vampire. Just take the role of the Count in a creepy skit that looks just like an old-time vampire movie!

You will need:
- your party gang
- markers
- cardboard signs
- a few flashlights
- some audience participation

Here's what you do:
1. Turn out all the lights.
2. Ask the actors to stand on stage (or in the front of the room, if you don't happen to have a stage in your house).
3. Have the members of the audience turn on their flashlights and point them at the actors. Then the audience members should wave their flashlights up and down really fast. The flickering of the flash-lights will make the actors' movements look like an old-fashioned movie. (If you have a tape of some creepy music, that will also help set a spooky mood.)

Here's an idea for a funny skit you can perform. And, of course, you can come up with lots of your own ideas. But remember, this is a silent movie. The actors don't talk. They can, however, hold up signs that represent the things they wish to say.

Vampire Vacation

The cast:
- A bat
- Count Dracula
- The Lovely Young Maiden
- The Card Holder

The Scene: Outside Dracula's Transylvanian Castle.

The Action: The Lovely Young Maiden is sitting alone, admiring the moonlight. The Card Holder walks in, holding a sign that says: "I am so glad I came to vacation here in Transylvania. It is so relaxing."

Suddenly, the Bat flies in. He hovers near the Lovely Young Maiden, who looks up and opens her mouth to scream. The Card Holder walks in holding a sign that says "AAAAAH! A BAT!"

The Lovely Young Maiden tries to run, but the

Bat blocks her path. He bends down and kneels at her feet. Suddenly the Card Holder walks in, holding a sign that says, "If you like *bats,* you're gonna have a *ball* with this guy." (Have the person playing Count Dracula sneak on stage by hiding behind the Card Holder.)

Now the Card Holder should block the audience's view of the Bat. That's because you're about to perform some movie magic. Suddenly, Count Dracula will jump out from his hiding place behind the Card Holder. The Bat will then hide behind the Card Holder and both will move off stage. If you time this just right, it will appear that the Bat has become Count Dracula.

The Count comes up behind the Lovely Young Maiden. The Card Holder reappears holding a sign that says, "I am Count Dracula. Welcome to my humble home. It is just the right place for someone who likes to take a *bite* out of life!"

The Count then sneaks up behind the Lovely Young Maiden and pretends to sink his teeth into her neck. The Card Holder appears again, holding a sign that says "Yum! AB negative. A rare delicacy!"

The Lovely Young Maiden falls to the ground. The Count bends down and helps her to her feet. The Card Holder returns with a card that reads "RUN FOR IT!"

Then, in a flash, the Count and the Lovely Young Maiden race into the audience, searching for fresh blood!

Great job as Count Dracula, kid. You're *almost* ready to become a vampire. But first, a few more jokes!

Super Spooky Joke Stop #3!

How can you tell if a vampire has a cold?
The vampire starts coffin!

What's the best way to phone a vampire?
Long distance!

Why did the vampires cancel their baseball game?
They couldn't find their bats!

Congratulations, kid!

You have successfully completed your vampire training. I am going to turn you into a vampire for all eternity. Now, hold still and tilt your head back so I can get a look at that neck.

Don't worry, kid. This won't hurt—too much.

Wait a minute. What's that? What's that coming through the window?

No! It can't be! It can't be morning already!

The sun! I can't stand the sun!

Noooooo!

THE END